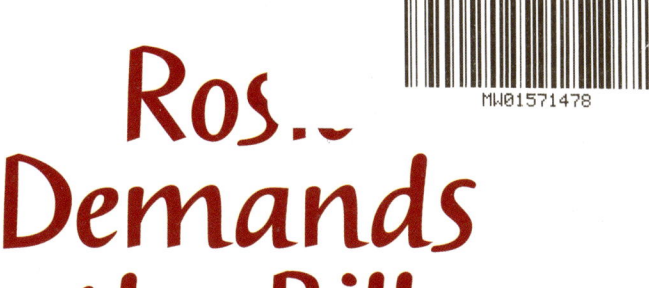

Rosie Demands the Bill

Story by Pamela Rushby
Illustrations by Paul Könye

Contents

Chapter 1	Lee's Turn	2
Chapter 2	Lee's Grandmother	6
Chapter 3	Rosie Meets Mrs Chen	14
Chapter 4	Too Noisy!	18

Chapter 1

Lee's Turn

"When do you want us to bring Rosie to your apartment?" Grace asked Lee. "It's your turn to look after her, now."

"I'm not sure," said Lee.

"We'd better wait until Mr Grimm goes out," Ahmed said, "because you live across the hall from him."

"We sure don't want Mr Grimm to see Rosie!" Jack said. "You know what he'd say – no pets!"

Lee's Turn

"We can borrow my sister's pram again," Ahmed said. "Then Mr Grimm won't see Rosie."

Lee didn't say anything.

"So, are you ready to look after Rosie?" Jack asked Lee.

"Mmm. . . ," said Lee.

Grace looked at Lee. "What's wrong? Rosie's wing is a lot better. She doesn't need much looking after."

"It's not that," said Lee.

"Well, what is it?" said Jack.

"It's my dad," Lee said. "He says my gran might be afraid of parrots."

Chapter 2
Lee's Grandmother

The children looked at each other. They'd all met Mrs Chen, Lee's grandmother. She'd come from China to live with Lee's family just a few months ago. Lee's gran had never left China before. She didn't speak very much English. She hardly ever left the Chens' apartment. She sat in her room and read books and watched videos most of the day.

Lee's Grandmother

"She's very homesick," Lee said, "so she hardly ever smiles."

"Maybe she'll like Rosie," Grace said.

"If she doesn't, then I can have Rosie!" Jack said quickly.

Lee's Grandmother

Lee glared at him. "I want to have my turn!" he said.

"Fine," Jack said. "Let's get Rosie to your place, then."

Rosie Demands the Bill

The children waited until they saw Mr Grimm go out. Then they put Rosie's cage in Ahmed's little sister's pram and went in the lift down to Lee's apartment. The lift doors opened on the ground floor.

"Oh, no!" Ahmed said.

Mr Grimm was coming in the front door.

"What are you children up to now?" he said. "You're not playing in the lift, I hope!"

"Oh, no," said Grace. "We're looking after Rosie again."

"That's all right, then," said Mr Grimm.

Lee's Grandmother

Lee pushed the pram across the hall to his apartment and the others followed.

Lee's dad, Mr Chen, looked hard at Rosie. "I hope she's not going to be a nuisance," he said. "Does she make much noise? You know I need to sleep during the day, Lee."

Rosie looked at Mr Chen. She put her head on one side. "Cup of tea?" she said. "Bill?"

Mr Chen laughed. "Well, that's good! When you own a restaurant, you always like someone who asks for the bill! I just don't know if my mother will like her, though."

"Let's show her!" said Jack.

Lee's Grandmother

Chapter 3

Rosie Meets Mrs Chen

The children carried Rosie's cage to Mrs Chen's room. Mrs Chen was sitting in her room, pouring pale green tea into a little cup with no handle. She looked tired and sad.

"What's that?" Grace asked Lee.

"It's Chinese tea," Lee said. "My gran likes it."

"Cup of tea?" said Rosie loudly. "Bill?"

"Well, Rosie seems to like it, too!" said Ahmed.

"Oh!" said Lee's gran, looking at Rosie. "Oh! Beautiful bird!"

She said something in Chinese and smiled.

"Well, my mother seems to like Rosie," Mr Chen said. "That's good."

Rosie Meets Mrs Chen

15

Rosie Demands the Bill

The children left Rosie with Lee's gran and went to the park to play. They could still hear Rosie saying, "Cup of tea? Bill?" when they were out in the hall. Mrs Chen was talking to her in Chinese.

When they came back from the park, Mr Chen was sitting in the kitchen with his head in his hands. In Mrs Chen's room, Rosie was still calling, "Cup of tea?" and Mrs Chen was talking to her.

Rosie Meets Mrs Chen

"Cup of tea?"
"Bill?"

Chapter 4

Too Noisy!

"Shouldn't you be in bed, Dad?" asked Lee. "You're working tonight, aren't you?"

"In bed!" said Mr Chen. "Who can sleep with that noise going on? It's like someone ordering tea and asking for the bill at the restaurant – but it's going on all day!"

"Rosie never talked so much at my place," said Grace.

"It's my mother," said Mr Chen. "She's talking to Rosie. I'm glad she's happy, but it's so noisy!"

"If Rosie talks this much, Mr Grimm might hear her," said Ahmed.

There was a knock on the door. Mr Chen opened it.

There was Mr Grimm!

"Someone's complained about the noise from this apartment," he said. "What's going on?"

The children stood in a frightened group. Was Mr Grimm going to find Rosie?

Lee's gran peeked out the door of her room. She saw Mr Grimm. "Video!" she said to Mr Grimm. "Very good program! Come in – listen!"

"A video – is that all?" Mr Grimm said. "Well, that's all right. Please just turn it down a little."

After Mr Grimm left the apartment, Lee hugged his gran. "Thanks for not telling Mr Grimm about Rosie," he said.

"Very beautiful bird," said Mrs Chen. She gave the children a big smile.

Too Noisy!

"I'm sorry, Lee," Mr Chen said. "Rosie will have to go. I can't sleep — and Mr Grimm will be back again."

"Then it's my turn to have Rosie!" Jack said.

Rosie Demands the Bill